ELEGY

FOR

KOSOVO

ELEGY
FOR
KOSOVO

ISMAIL KADARE

TRANSLATED FROM THE ALBANIAN
BY PETER CONSTANTINE

ARCADE PUBLISHING • NEW YORK

First published in France under the title *Trois chants funèbras pour le Kosovo* in 1998 by Librairie Arthème Fayard.

Original title in Albanian: *Tri Këngë zie për Kosovën*

Arcade Publishing books may be purchased in bulk at special discounts for sales promotion, corporate gifts, fund-raising, or educational purposes. Special editions can also be created to specifications. For details, contact the Special Sales Department, Arcade Publishing, 307 West 36th Street, 11th Floor, New York, NY 10018 or arcade@skyhorsepublishing.com.

Arcade Publishing® is a registered trademark of Skyhorse Publishing, Inc.®, a Delaware corporation.

Visit our website at www.arcadepub.com.

10 9 8 7 6 5 4 3 2 1

Library of Congress Cataloging-in-Publication Data is available on file.

ISBN: 978-1-61145-697-4

Printed in China

Contents

The Ancient Battle

I

Never before had rumors of impending war been followed by rumors of peace. Quite the opposite — after hopes for peace, suddenly war would be declared, which was practically routine in the large peninsula.

There were times when the peninsula seemed truly large, with enough space for everyone: for different languages and faiths, for a dozen peoples, states, kingdoms, and principalities — even for three empires, two of which, the Serbian and the Bulgarian, were now in ruins, with the result that the third, the Byzantine Empire, was to its disgrace and that of all Christianity declared a Turkish vassal.

But times changed, and with them the ideas of the local people changed, and the peninsula began to seem quite constricting. This feeling of constriction was spawned more by the ancient memories of the people than by their lands and languages rubbing against each other. In their solitude the people hatched nightmares until one day they felt they could no longer bear it.

This usually happened in the spring, when, along with the whispers of war or peace, there was a feeling of inexplicable tension in the air. In fact, both the good and the bad prophecies never ebbed in the low-lying regions, particularly in the towns. But they tended to become a flood when they mingled with the anxiety of the mountain people. And this happened in the spring, right after the first signs of the snow melting. The explanation was simple enough: the predictions of the city people were based on information and rumors spread by itinerant merchants, consuls' coachmen, spies, epileptics, and harbor prostitutes, and on the rate of exchange of Venetian ducats in the Durrës banks. Nonetheless, however reliable these sources of information might be, another dimension was necessary to authenticate such rumors, a dimension that was mysterious and intangible — in other words, irrational. This dimension was provided by the mountain people.

For the mountain people, everything from the Cursed Peaks of Albania and Montenegro to ancient Mount Olympus and the Carpathians was linked with snow. Just as the city people imagined a world that was basically flat, the people of the mountain pastures made the opposite mistake; they believed in the supremacy of the mountains. So even if somebody swore a solemn oath that he had seen with his own eyes an army ready for war, the mountain people would look up toward the snows and shake their heads. As long as the cherished snow still lay up there, no army was on the move, no war was about to begin.

In the spring this conviction was shattered, and with the melting snow thoughts changed.

This is what happened in that spring of 1389 when, right after the news that there would be a very special peace, there came other news that there would be war, and that this war would be very special indeed.

II

*T*hat spring the world was rife with rumors. No caravan transporting cheeses, no consul passing through could fill the emptiness — it filled itself spontaneously. People had also realized in recent years that where the roads were blocked by snow or plague, the whispers, instead of dying away, became even stronger. The reason seems to have been that the lack of fresh news made people turn to the past. The news of what had gone before, like old clothing, was easier to slip into.

In remote taverns they spoke of the Turks moving their capital from Bursa to Adrianople, as if the event had occurred the day before and not some twenty years earlier. And that the Turkish monarch was moving the capital, some said, in order to shift his empire to Europe. Others either refused to believe this or shook their heads in horror. Can one move an empire as if it were a house? Not to mention: Where would poor Europe find enough space for such a huge empire? The Turk doesn't give a damn if it fits or not. "Move over!" he says. "Make room for me, or I'll kick you out!"

Others, who did not want to believe that this calamity could come about, said that if the sultan was moving the capital nearer, it was perhaps so that it would be easier for him to keep an eye on the quarrels of the peninsula's princes. "To keep an eye on our wrangling?" others objected incredulously. "Our wrangling is so deafening that there is no need to come closer — in fact you can hear it better from afar!"

The discussion about the quarrels of the native princes turned spontaneously to their secret alliances, particularly their bondage to the

Turk. Of all the rumors, these were the most unsubstantiated. No sooner did word go around that King Tvrtko of the Bosnians had bowed down to the sultan, than other news came that it wasn't King Tvrtko, nor Mirçea of Rumania, but Sisman, czar of the Bulgarians, who had knelt before the sultan. "I am not surprised about the Bulgarian czar," an unknown man said, "but my soul aches when I call to mind Emperor John V!"

"Ah, Byzantium!" others sighed. "Byzantium, my friend! You have sinned and now you must pay the price."

The news that people were wrangling not only here in this godforsaken part of the world but everywhere, even among the Turks themselves, was a consolation. Everyone was talking about the affair of the two princes, the Turk Cuntuz, son of Sultan Murad, and Andronicus, the heir of John V. While the fathers had formed an alliance and were busy waging war in Asia, the sons were conspiring to overthrow them. The fathers clapped them in irons, and Sultan Murad, in order to reaffirm his friendship with his Christian ally, had his treacherous son punished with the official Byzantine torture — blinding. And, needless to say, the Christian monarch reciprocated with *his* son.

Talking about the savagery of these two fathers reminded people of their evils and caprices. Many of these monarchs' actions, which seemed to defy reason, were beyond understanding not because they were inscrutable but because of their inherent madness. The idea of moving the capital, for instance, might well have had a sound motive but was more likely the outcome of one of the sultan's whims. With an empire of such boundless proportions, such whims were to be expected. Too often the great are permitted what lesser men are not. The Montenegrins might have liked to move their capital, Cetinje, but where would they have put it? Two miles over, and the wretched city would have landed in the talons of the Albanian eagle. The same goes for Skopje, and as for Sofia, God knows where it would have ended up! In Russia, probably, or in the Black Sea!

Twilight fell, and before the taverns closed and everyone wished each other a good night, the conversation turned to the latest piece of news — the Turkish monarch's change of title. Until recently, he had been called "Emir," but now he was going to be called "Sultan." This was definitely a bad sign. The last time there had been a change was on the threshold of a war. Besides which, the title "Emir" sounded tender to all ears — in the languages of the southern Slavs the word *mir* means *peace,* while in the language of the Albanians it sounds like *i mirë, good man,* or *e mirë, good woman.*

"And yet, did he not slash us all to pieces under that title at the battle of Maricë?" someone asked as he put on a skullcap. "Slashed us to pieces, by God!" said another, scratching his head. "And not only the Serbs and the Hungarians, but also we Albanians who had rushed off to help them, and even the French king,

Louis d'Anjou. It is where my lord Count Muzaka fell, may he rest in peace!"

"Sultan." The people muttered the new title to themselves as if they were trying to fathom its secret.

It was clear as the light of day that the Turkish monarch wished to adopt a new title, just as he had invented new weapons in the last couple of years, just as he had modernized the shape of the *yataghan* sabers and their curved blades.

In other words, new war, new name, the people said, and put a curse on him then and there: "May he not live to enjoy it!" and "May the title swallow him up!"

III

*E*ver since the Venetians began using mute couriers, political rumors, particularly those emanating from roadside inns, had fallen off considerably. But as is often the case when greed incites an individual or a state to foolish deeds, the Venetians were not satisfied with simple secrecy but strove to go even further. And since the only courier more secretive than one whose tongue has been cut out is a dead courier, the Venetians' quest moved in an unexpected direction. Their new couriers were not deaf-mutes and not blind mutes, as one would have expected, but normal couriers with eyes, ears, and tongues — in fact, tongues that wagged far more than usual. In short, the often gloomy and taciturn couriers of the past were replaced by talkative couriers who were eager to sit down for a good chat with any traveler they came across at wayside inns.

It wasn't all that difficult to guess that they had two types of information: true information, which they guarded carefully, and falsehoods, which they dropped in fragments over the course of an evening by the fireside, as if by a slip of the tongue or from too much drink.

That spring the false news was often enough injurious to the opposition, as was to be expected, but it often also came back to haunt those who had spread it. The road from the Turkish capital to Venice was long, and to carry both truths and lies at the same time was not easy. At times the truth and at times the lies would color each other, adding to the surrounding fog, which was heavy in the month of March.

It was common knowledge that letters were exchanged that had been written in six languages and four different alphabets. But what was written in these letters, the Lord alone knew. "Islam will come face to face with the Christian cross," the sultan had been said to proclaim in his message. "One or the other will succumb." But another source maintained the opposite: "There is no need to raise your weapons, my children! On earth as in Heaven, there is room enough for all — for your cross and our crescent."

Other rumors hinted at newly sealed alliances among the princes of the peninsula, and then, as was to be expected, newer rumors immediately announced their rupture. Envoys of the pope arrived in Durrës from Rome every week. Messengers set out from Belgrade to Walachia. "I am bringing with me my two sons, Yakub Çelebi and Bayezid," the sultan was said to have written in his letter. "Bring your sons as well. Either you will extinguish my line completely, or I shall extinguish yours." "What about your third son, the one you blinded, Cuntuz? Why will you not bring him too?" "I would love to bring him, upon my Faith! But what am I to do? — Allah has called him to His side."

It was said that the Albanian princes had allied themselves with Lazar of the Serbs and Tvrtko of the Bosnians. Emperor John V was wavering, and there was still no word from Prince Constantine. Nor from Mirçea of Rumania. As for the other Serb, Marko Kraljevic, all the omens showed that he was preparing for a new betrayal.

"My greetings to you! I hope that we shall come to an agreement!"

"So come, and may you never leave again!"

"I shall come, I shall find you, and I shall cover you with earth!"

"It would be better for all concerned if we could reach an agreement about where we are to meet. Why tire ourselves out by hunting each other down in vain? On the Plains of Nish, or on the Field of the Blackbirds, Kosovo, as you call it."

"Go to the devil, Sultan Murad!"

IV

*T*he Turkish capital was bustling with preparations. The army's vanguard had already set out, and the sultan's younger son, Bayezid, begged his father to take elephants along, but the monarch refused. His other son, Yakub, was expected to arrive any day now with vassals gathered from far and wide. More than forty honey merchants were beaten with sticks in the market square for having tried to cheat during the weighing of the honey destined for the army. "Shame! Shame!" the crowd shouted. To swindle with the honey that will give soldiers strength as they go to battle, and that might very well turn out to be their last meal in this world, was truly an infamy.

The royal chief historian was dismissed for having begun his war chronicle with the very same words that he had used some years earlier for the military campaign against the emir of the Karamans: "Our illustrious Grand Sovereign, Light of the World, was in his garden harking to the song of the birds when the message came unto him that the infidels were preparing an insurrection." His rival, who had waited twenty years to supplant him, spent a sleepless week contriving *his* introduction, which differed only slightly from his predecessor's: "Our superbly illustrious Grand Sovereign, the Light of our Universe, was in his garden harking to the murmuring of the fountains when the message came unto him that the infidels were preparing an insurrection." He, too, was dismissed, and even beaten with a stick, as were all the other candidates, while everyone waited for a Jewish historian from Erzurum, of whom it was said that he had lost his mind one day but that it had come back and was even more brilliant than before. In the meantime, in his gigantic chamber, Sultan Murad stood before a map of Europe, listening to the explanations of his pasha of the seas: "Europe is like a bad-tempered mule, Grand Sovereign, and these three peninsulas dangling down there are like three little bells. Once we have silenced the first, the Balkan lands, we shall attack the second, Italy, land of the cross and the infidel. And then we shall strike the third bell, the land of the Spaniards, where Islam once reigned but was driven out."

The peninsula was preparing itself to confront the onslaught with just as much commotion. Weapon forges and taverns stayed open late into the night. Dignitaries tied and untied allegiances. Bellies were eager to be impregnated. The last weddings were held, and, as the war could start at any moment, the procession of the groom's family coming for the bride would march with banners so that the men would be ready at a moment's notice to change course if there should be a call to arms.

The minstrels had already begun to compose

their songs, each in his own language. They resembled the ancient songs; even the words were not that different. The Serbian elders chanted: "Oh, the Albanians are preparing to attack!" and the Albanian *lahuta*[1] minstrels sang: "Men, to arms! The pernicious Serb is upon us!"

"Are you out of your minds or are you making fools of us?" the people asked. "The Turks are marching on us, and you are singing the same old songs — 'The Serbs are attacking, the Albanians are attacking!' " "We know, we know!" the minstrels answered. "But this is where we've always turned to find parts for our songs, and this is where we will always turn. These parts are not like those of weapons that change every ten years. Our models need at least a century to adapt!"

In the meantime, the Ottoman army had already set out, and truths and untruths were spawned. But there was something that unsettled

---

[1] A bowed, single-string northern Albanian instrument with an egg-shaped body and long neck.

the people of the peninsula even more than the approaching army: the word *Balkan*. Before the Turks even set foot on the peninsula, they baptized it and its people with this name, and this name stuck to them like new scales on the body of an aged reptile. The people were at their wits' end. They twisted in their sleep as if they were trying to shake off this name, but the result was the opposite — the name clung to them all the more forcefully, as if it wanted to become one with their skin. They now realized that, divided as they had always been, they had never given their peninsula a name. Some had called it "Illyricum," some "New Byzantium"; others had opted for "Alpania" because of the peninsula's alps, or "Great Slavonia" because of the Slavs, and so on. Now it was too late to do anything, and so, without a common name but with a name bestowed upon them by the enemy, they marched to battle and defeat.

V

*T*he imperial Turkish army did not surface in Nish, as had been expected, but headed for the Plains of Kosovo. The Balkan princes rushed there like wild torrents that change their course after a storm. When they arrived, the Turks were already waiting. The Balkan army positioned itself across from them on the side of the plain that the Turks had deliberately left open for them. Tvrtko of the Bosnians was the only king among them, but Prince Lazar of the Serbs was elected commander in chief, as he had the greatest number of troops. To his left were the battalions of Mirçea of Rumania, and to his right the Albanian counts Gjergj Balsha and Demetër Jonima with their soldiers. There were also other battalions, which had arrived over the past few days. Some thought they might be Croat, others Hungarian, but like so much else in this war, no one was certain what they were.

Facing the Balkan army, alongside the Turks and their Asian vassals, were the troops of Prince Constantine and the traitor Marko Kraljevic. Absent — though no one knew why — was John V of Byzantium.

It was late June. The day seemed to last forever, the afternoon even more so. When it seemed that the waiting would never stop, the Turks lit wet straw in front of their tents, creating a wall of smoke. The Balkan troops did the same, each side to shield their opponents from view, showing that they could no longer bear the sight of each other. Or, they wanted to hide something.

When night finally came, it seemed darker because of the long wait. Now that the two sides could no longer see each other, they grew increasingly anxious instead of calming down. Everything their eyes had seen that long afternoon became larger and more frightening: the expanse of the Turkish encampment, the myriad banners of the Balkan troops, the conjectures in the ubiquitous darkness as to where the sultan's tent might be.

As if to precipitate an answer to this last question, Mirçea of Rumania lit a fire next to his tent. The other princes followed suit, but the sultan's tent remained steeped in darkness. Nor did the shouts of the Balkan troops provoke a response on the other side. Except for the wailing voices of the muezzins, which the Balkans now heard for the first time and which seemed to them like a deadly lullaby, no sound came from the Turkish camp.

Provoked by this, the Balkan soldiers, who had sworn before their council that they would not drink wine, especially on the eve of the battle, broke their resolve. First the princes, then the other commanders, sent each other gifts of wine, and then, after the exchange of wine, they took their guards and their minstrels, which each had brought from his own land to sing his glory on the morrow, and went to visit their allies in their tents.

They did not hide that they were certain of victory, that they could not wait for the sun to rise; some even wanted to attack before the break of day. A few of the commanders were already busy calculating how many slaves they would each get and at which market they could be sold for the greatest profit — in Venice or Dubrovnik — and all the while the minstrels sang their ancient songs without changing anything, as was their custom. The Serb prince, Lazar, and the Albanian count, Gjergj Balsha, laughed out loud when they heard the Serbian *gusla*[2] player — "Rise, O Serbs! The Albanians are taking Kosovo from us!" — and

---

[2] A Montenegrin bowed string instrument.

the Albanian lahuta player — "Albanians, to arms! The pernicious Serb is seizing Kosovo!"

"This is how things come to pass in this world," one of the princes is supposed to have said. "Blood flows one way in life and another way in song, and one never knows which flow is the right one."

VI

*P*rince Bayezid could not fall asleep. Finally he got up and went outside his tent. From far away the wind brought waves of boisterous din from the Balkan side. "What a horror!" he said to himself and tried to make out in which direction his father's tent lay.

"You are not tired?" It was the gentle voice of Anastasios, his Greek tutor. Wrapped in a heavy woolen cloak, he sat to the left of the sentries like a tree stump. "Besides the soldiers who are really asleep, there are those tonight who are merely feigning sleep."

"You think so?" the prince said. "I did manage to catch a few winks; I even had a mad half dream. This cursed clamor seems to have awakened me."

"Hmm," his tutor said. "It has come to my attention that the young officers, even some of the viziers, have been somewhat unsettled at the sight of the Balkan troops."

"That is to be expected," Bayezid said. "Many of them have never come face to face with a Christian army."

"Perhaps the order to raise the curtain of smoke was given too late," the tutor replied.

"Much too late!" the prince said. "To tell you the truth, even though I was fully aware it was only a Christian army, I myself felt somewhat disconcerted."

"I know what you mean," Anastasios said. He coughed several times, as if he wanted to give his voice the unwavering resonance of the bygone days when he had recounted ancient tales and legends to the young prince. It was a distinctive way of speaking that flowed with conviction, not allowing for the slightest interruption. "You are unsettled by the wild jumble of their troops, my prince. All those banners and icons and crosses and multicolored emblems, and the trumpets, and the long and resonant names and titles of their dukes and counts, and then the musicians and poets poised to sing the glory of each and every one of them for generations to come. I fully understand you, my prince, especially when you compare that wild jumble to the dusty monotony of our army. I understand you, but let us wait till tomorrow, my prince. Tomorrow you shall see that the real instrument of war is not theirs, but ours — dusty and drab like mud, with a single banner, a single commander, and no emblems or flamboyant poets, no commanders thirsting for glory or sporting long titles, names, and surnames. Obedient, sober, mute, and nameless like mud — that is the army of the future, my prince. The day before we marched off I happened to look through the rosters of our soldiers. The majority were listed only by their forenames — no distinguishing features, not even a surname.

More than thirteen hundred Abdullahs, nine hundred Hassans, a thousand or so Ibrahims, and so on. It is these shadows, as they might appear to an onlooker, who will face those strutting Balkans and slash their names, their long peacock-tail titles, and ultimately slash their lives. Mark my words, Prince!"

He went on speaking for quite a long time, and Bayezid, just as when he was a boy, did not interrupt him. The Greek said that the Ottoman army was uniform, that it had an unfathomable face, he said, like that of Allah. The Christians had lost their future ever since they had given a human likeness — Christ — to their God. There were times when the Christians tried to mend their error by melting away his face and transforming it into a cross, but it was too late.

Anastasios sighed. After so many years he had earned the right to show his regret at the defeat of Christianity, his own faith. He wanted to tell the prince that if there was a power in the world that they should be afraid of, it wasn't foolish Europe but the Mongolian hordes. They were even more nameless, and therefore even more apocalyptic. It would be like being attacked by the wild weeds and thorns of the steppes. But Anastasios said nothing, because he did not want to demoralize the prince on the eve of the battle.

"You must rest now," he told him, peering at the horizon for the first signs of dawn. "If I am not mistaken, tomorrow — that is to say, today — you will be leading the right flank of the army."

"That is true," the prince replied.

The prince turned around and walked to his tent, but before entering it he turned back again and, with a low, timid voice, almost like when all those years ago he had confessed his sin and spoken of his first temptation with a woman, he said to his tutor:

"Anastasios, why . . . despite everything, am I entranced by . . . their madness?"

His tutor did not answer immediately. He stood for a moment with his head bowed, as if a heavy rock, not a thought, had entered his brain.

"This means that new ideas are being generated in your head," he said in a muted voice. "But tonight is not the right time, Prince. You must rest at all costs. Tomorrow . . ."

He did not manage to finish his sentence, as Bayezid had already slipped into his tent.

VII

*T*he day was coming to an end, and with it came the end of the Balkan troops. Several times fate appeared to smile on them, only to immediately abandon them. They followed all the rules: they had invoked spells, made ancient signs of death, blown trumpets, chanted hymns to Christ and the Virgin Mary, and then sung praises to Prince Lazar and maledictions on Kraljevic the traitor, and then again praises to the other princes, to the Rumanian chiefs, the counts, and King Tvrtko, and curses on those who pretended to be more heroic than they. Finally, when they saw that all this was of no avail, they began to cheer on holy Serbia, glorious Walachia, Bosnia the immortal, Albania begot by an eagle, and so on, but it was too late for all of this, too. The Turks facing them, who had never seen anything like this before, charged, shouting only the name of Allah, in the simple conviction that they had come here to take this evil region, which was a blot, a scandal on the face of the earth, and bring it back to the right path; in other words, to make it an Islamic region.

In the boundless confusion, it was the Balkan troops who faltered. One after the other, banners with their crosses, lions, one-headed and two-headed eagles fell, and finally the banners with white lilies fell, as if they had fallen on a graveyard. Torrents of Christian and Turkish blood mingled more forcefully than they would have in a thousand years of intermarriage.

In the twilight, when victory was certain, Sultan Murad decided to rest a while. He had not slept for such a long time that even the taste of victory was as acrid as a bitter potion.

Outside, cheers of triumph came from afar.

"I shall doze a little," the monarch said, and when the viziers told him that his soldiers wanted to see him, even just for a moment, he cut them short. "Send them my double."

They gazed at their sovereign with flashing feverish eyes, not like his eyes, which were hazy from lack of rest.

The sultan immediately fell asleep. He had a dream in which an officer or a cook who had been dead for some time was complaining to him about something.

"I don't understand what you are saying," the sultan said. "You are dead, dead and gone, it's all over and done with!"

"I am not asking you for anything important, no," the man answered. "It's just the wound that I have, bad and crooked as it is — how am I supposed to bear it throughout death? I wanted to fix it, but you didn't take me along with you to the Plains of Kosovo."

The sultan wanted to tell him, "What strange ideas, my dear fellow!" But the man continued,

"Be that as it may, the best have died. They have also killed your double. Be careful, my lord!"

He spoke the last words in a different voice. The sultan opened his eyes. He heard the words again, but this time not from the dead man but from his viziers.

"Your double has been killed, Grand Sovereign. A Balkan infidel . . . hurled himself on him . . . onto his horse, like a wild cat."

The sultan shook his head to wake up. It was true, there they were, dragging the body of his double to the entrance of the tent. He was wearing the sultan's heavy wool cloak, his plumes and emblems, and right in the center, the dagger planted in his heart.

The sultan looked at him, taken aback for a moment. "My death," he thought, "but outside myself." He raised his eyes and looked at his viziers, amazed that they did not congratulate him on his escape. He wanted to ask them: "Why are you standing there like that? Are you so distraught at the death of my double?" And he looked back down at the corpse. He remembered an ancient proverb that when the oak tree falls its shadow falls with it, and he wasn't sure whether the proverb had conjured itself up in his memory or if he had just heard one of his viziers say it. For a split second he thought that the officer or cook was reappearing in the drowsiness that was once more overpowering him. Before he lost consciousness, he heard the grand vizier speak: "Bring his son, Prince Yakub! Tell him that his illustrious father wishes to see him."

He struggled to open his mouth, and with his entire strength and with all his impatient fury and rage wanted to howl, "Why Yakub? Why my eldest son?"

REPORT OF THE SECRET ENVOY TO THE
PLAINS OF KOSOVO.
TO BE PLACED SOLELY IN THE HANDS OF
HIS HOLINESS THE POPE.

As you will already have been informed, the Battle of Kosovo is over. Charles VI of France was in too much of a hurry to sing the victory *Te Deum* in the cathedral of Notre Dame in Paris. The defeat of our Christian allies was total. Within ten hours the Balkan wall fell, and Christianity has been left open to the wrath of the Ottomans.

The greatest defeat was suffered by the Serbs. Their Prince Lazar and his sons were taken captive. The other allies, the king of Bosnia, the Walachian lord, the Albanian counts, and the Hungarian and Croat boyars were completely routed.

It seemed as if fate wanted to offer a consolation to the defeated by murdering Sultan Murad I, but Heaven's intervention came far too late. All it did was make the river of blood flow more strongly. Before the sultan's martyred body they held a *kurban* — that is what they call sacrifices — the like of which has never before been seen. They slaughtered thousands of prisoners like cattle, among them Prince Lazar of the Serbs with his sons and dozens of other boyars.

Yakub Çelebi, the sultan's oldest son, was also killed, and his younger brother Bayezid was declared sultan.

A great enigma is connected with the Turkish sultan's death. It arose right after the murder, even before night had fallen. There are two versions of how he was killed. In the first, he died in his tent during the last moments of the battle, struck by a Balkan dagger. In the second, he was killed after the battle, while he was on horseback surveying the bloody battlefield, again struck by a Balkan dagger. Both versions are quite suspect. The first, the one with the tent, is extremely implausible; anyone with even a perfunctory knowledge of Turkish customs would be aware that no one could possibly approach the sultan's tent, especially not during battle. As for the second version, in which he was murdered as he rode his horse — this is no less suspect. First, how could a Balkan soldier lying among the dead get up and approach the sultan, who was on horseback, surrounded, as everyone is aware, by a great number of guards? Another even more difficult question is how the killer could have leaped up from the ground with lightning speed, reached the sultan's horse, and with the single stab of a dagger manage to strike the sultan's heart or throat, when it is obvious that even the simplest breastplate, let alone the breastplate of a sultan, would have made that impossible.

But all the aforementioned suspicions are dwarfed by a much graver question. In that blood-drenched twilight, right after the death of the sultan, the viziers convened to avert a struggle for power between the two princes and cold-bloodedly killed one of them. The following question remains: Why did they kill the sultan's older son, Yakub Çelebi, his legal heir, and not his younger son, Bayezid?

All the evidence points to the fact that the Turkish sultan was probably not killed by the Balkans but by his own people under mysterious circumstances, possibly as the result of a secret conspiracy that had been hatched some time previously. This seems to have resulted from two factions that had recently surfaced in the palace: one faction insisting that the empire center itself in Asia, the other that it expand westward. Since, according to facts already verified, Prince Yakub, like his father, supported the Asian faction, both his murder and that of his father point to political intrigue. From this standpoint, the assassination of the sultan and the heir apparent has been to our disadvantage, because it has opened the way for Ottoman aggression against us.

SUPPLEMENT TO THE REPORT

The above statement is further validated by the symbolism behind the sultan's partial interment on the Plains of Kosovo. The bizarre decision that the monarch's body be taken to the Ottoman capital but that his blood and intestines should be buried in the Christian soil of Kosovo has a clear significance. As is commonly known, the ancient Balkan people believed that everything linked with blood is eternal, imperishable, and guarded by fate. The Turks, who had at that point interacted with the Balkan people for over half a century, had apparently assimilated some of this symbolism. By pouring the monarch's blood on the Plains of Kosovo, they wanted to give that plain, just as they had done with the invasion, a direction, a fatality, both a curse and blessing at the same time; in other words, a "program," as one would call it today.

The Great Lady

I

*H*e had never before been on the losing side in a war, but nevertheless, late that afternoon, the first cracks began to appear. He closed his eyes wearily, but when he opened them again the view was still the same: soldiers and officers spinning in all directions as if caught up in a whirlwind. Two or three times he heard his name being shouted — Gjorg Shkreli! — but he was quick to realize that it was just his imagination. He didn't recognize a single person in the confusion — he had lost sight of his Albanians since noon. On a battlefield the minstrels are always the last to fall, Prince Lazar had said the preceding night, and gave the order that they should all

gather on a small mound not far from his tent —
the Serbs with their guslas, the Walachians and
the Bosnians with their flutes, and the players
of the one-string lahuta from the Cursed Peaks —
so that they could all follow the battle without
risking their heads. "Those minstrels have always
been the darlings of fate!" one of the men said
with a faint smile and a twinkle of envy in his
eyes, but the prince was quick to point out, "If we
lose them, who will sing our glory?"

All afternoon the minstrels stood outside the
commander in chief's tent, their eyes at times
clouded with tears as they watched the troop
movements.

A scorching blanket of heat lay over the Plains
of Kosovo, immersing them in a harsh, dreadful
light. In the crazed glare the movements of the
troops did not seem to make sense. The minstrels
heard shouts of triumph from the commander in
chief's tent when, under the pressure of the Christian forces, the center of the Turkish lines started
to bend back like a bow. The shouts came several

times, but the minstrels could not figure out what was happening. With eyes grown weary from the light they struggled to follow the movement of the banners bearing crosses that were being slashed to pieces by the Turkish crescent. The harsh light spread a great dread. Just as the intoxicating wine had the night before. "They are advancing too far!" an old Bosnian minstrel said. The preceding night he had warned that no one must drink before going into battle, not even princes.

More shouts came from Prince Lazar's tent as a horde of Serbs on horseback came thundering past. The soldiers following them told the minstrels the reason for the jubilation: the horses' hooves were covered in honey and rice — the Christian army had cut so deep into Turkish lines that it had reached its rear guard and crushed the barrels containing their provisions.

Here and there shouts of triumph could be heard, but Gjorg Shkreli could not shake off his apprehension. And always that harsh, intoxicating light that would not leave him in peace.

He soon noticed that he was not the only one to be uneasy. The horses of the heroes who had just been cheered seemed suddenly to slow down, hobbled by the honey as they stumbled back in the direction from which they had just come.

He stared again at the swirling banners over the swarm of soldiers. And it was in the sky that he thought he noticed the first sign of disaster. The silk of the banners was faltering and the crosses and the ornate lions and the crowned eagles no longer showed their former conviction. But the Ottoman crescents were rising with greater force. He could not escape the childish, illogical thought of how these lunar crescents, so undaunted by the blinding sun, would really come into their own as night fell.

There was a clamor to the right of Prince Lazar's tent, but with his attention focused on the battlefield Gjorg did not manage to turn around in time. It was only when he heard someone shout — "The commander in chief is moving out!" — that he realized what had happened.

"What about us?" Vladan, the Serbian minstrel, called out. "What are we supposed to do?"

The prince was not setting out on a glorious counterattack. He was relocating his camp, but nobody was prepared to tell the minstrels what this meant.

Gjorg tried to bolster himself with the idea that a commander in chief's relocation during a battle was nothing out of the ordinary, but his anxiety did not diminish.

The prince's empty tent was filled with the wounded. The cries grew ever louder. The minstrels began running about in panic, clutching their instruments, which had suddenly become a burden.

"I'm going to see if I can find my Walachians!" one of them shouted.

The other minstrels immediately began scouring the battlefield, searching for their banners.

Vladan's eyes filled with tears. It came as no surprise that people should be left behind in this confusion, he thought, but surely not a Serb of his distinction, who had stood outside the tent of Prince Lazar.

Gjorg, like the other minstrels, was also peering at the banners, looking for the Albanian eagles. He cursed himself for not having watched Count Balsha's troop movements on the plain, or at least those of Jonima. Now it was too late to find them.

The drums of the two sides were still beating. Gjorg finally made out the Albanian banners, but their black and white eagles seemed harried, as if chased by a thunderstorm.

"Protect us, Mary Mother of God!" he silently prayed.

He started retreating like the others, without knowing where to. Someone shouted: "The Turks are attacking from this side!" Others shouted words that might have been taken for orders but quickly changed into laments. Again he lost sight of the banners with the Albanian eagles, but still he continued moving. "What a calamity!" someone shouted. "Turn back!" another yelled, but no one knew anymore which way was forward and which was back. King Tvrtko's banner veered to the left of the battlefield. Then for an instant Prince Lazar's banner appeared in a dust cloud right next to the menacing crescents.

Everyone ran. Unknown men, short swords in hand, glared with wild eyes. Gjorg had lost all hope of finding his Albanians.

His mind a blank, he turned back to where he had just come from, to the abandoned tent of the commander in chief. He came face to face with Vladan. Vladan was sobbing, tearing at his hair: "Prince Lazar has been captured! Serbia is dead!"

"Jesus Christ protect us!" Gjorg said, and held out his hand to Vladan to steady him. They made their way through the total confusion, Vladan ranting deliriously. "I've lost my gusla! Perhaps I threw it away myself! I thought, what do I need it for! If Prince Lazar has been taken prisoner, we're all finished! Where are your Albanians?"

"I have no idea," Gjorg answered. "I can't even see our banners anymore!"

"There's no point looking for them! They've all fallen! Throw away your lahuta, brother! You won't want to be singing with the Turks!"

"Holy Mary!" Gjorg said. "I have never seen such a calamity in my life!"

Soldiers ran in all directions, gasping, stumbling over dead bodies. Men who had thrown away their weapons crouched down by corpses to snatch up their swords, only to throw them away again a few steps later. From all around men shouted: "Stop!" — "Where are you going?" — "Which side are you on?"

Through all the mayhem, shreds of violent news were heard. Mirçea of Rumania was heading for the Danube with his Walachians. King Tvrtko, having by now lost his crown, was hurrying back to Bosnia. The Catholic Albanians were following Count Balsha to the foggy mountains of western Albania, while the Orthodox

Albanians were following Jonima down to the Macedonian flatlands. Everyone but the dead was trying to escape from the cursed plain.

"I had a premonition in my heart!" Vladan murmured. "For days now, I have had a premonition in my heart of this great disaster!"

"Then why," Gjorg wanted to ask him, "why did you bring bad luck upon us, you wretch!" But he was too exhausted even to move his lips.

Hoarse voices came from far away: "Come back everyone! Good news! The Turkish sultan has been killed!"

Strangely enough, everyone kept running. They heard the news but had forgotten it in an instant. The day was coming to an end. It was too late to do anything. For a moment the fugitives glanced back at the wide plain, as if to sense where the sultan might have died, then right away, exhausted, they realized that his death, like everything else, had come too late.

Darkness fell quickly. There was a feeling that

this day, with its harsh, morbid brightness, could engender only an all-engulfing darkness. Through this darkness trudged officers who had torn off their insignia, now doubly hidden, and soldiers, cooks, carriers of secrets that no longer served a purpose, keepers of the official seal, assassins who had not been able to ply their trade, army clerics whose terror had driven them insane, and madmen whose terror had brought them back to sanity.

Twice Gjorg was tempted to throw away his lahuta, but both times he had thought he was going mad and changed his mind. If he could keep a clear head until morning, he would not go insane. The third time he thought of throwing away his lahuta, the instrument's single string gave off a mournful sound, as if to say, "What have I done to you?"

The fugitives made their way through the darkness like black beetles. Someone had lit a torch, and in its light the men's faces looked even more frightening. Dogs were licking the hooves of a fallen horse. "Lord in Heaven!" Gjorg muttered. "It is the honey we were cheering this very morning."

"We are dead, brother!" he heard Vladan's voice say. "Do you believe me now, that we are nothing but spirits?"

II

*T*hey had been walking for four days and no longer knew where they were. The throng of fugitives would swell and then thin out again in sorrow. Tagging along at times were Hungarian soldiers whose language nobody understood, Walachians desperately looking for the Danube, Jews who had come from God knows where. Just as suddenly as they had appeared, they disappeared again the following day, as if snatched away by some dream. A Turkish subaltern also tagged along for part of the way, the only Turk, it seemed, who had thrown in his lot with the Christians. He stared at everything in amazement, and every time they stopped to rest he would ask the others to teach him the correct way of crossing himself.

In a stupor, Gjorg heard snippets of conversation. "I think we've left Albania, we've been walking so many days now" — "I think so too" — "This isn't Serbian land" — "What do you think?" — "I'd say this isn't Serbia" — "What? Not Serbia, not Albania?" — "Let me put it to you this way, my friend: some say this is Serbia, some say Albania. The Lord only knows which of the two it really is. So who owns this accursed plain where we spilled our blood, the Field of the Blackbirds, as they call it? It was there, my brother, that the fighting started — a hundred, maybe even two hundred years ago."

Gjorg opened his eyes and thought he saw the Cursed Peaks. They were crowned by the snow and the sky he knew, but the villages at their foot were different. His eyes filled with tears at the thought that he might never see them again.

Gjorg had lost sight of his traveling companions, including Vladan. Two Albanians he met outside a village told him that they were on their way to Albania, but that they couldn't take him along. They were military couriers, and had to get there as fast as possible by whatever means they could — boat, cart, horses. They had to find their lord, Count Balsha, as soon as possible and hand him a message.

Gjorg didn't understand. The calamity must have driven them mad, for what kind of message could they be delivering now that the war was lost? And if it were such an urgent matter, then why were they dozens of miles astray, and how were they going to find the count? How did they even know he was alive, and what could the point of such a message be, now that everyone was dead?

They listened coldly to his questions and told him that they were military couriers, that they were not permitted to question or doubt. It had been in the course of that horrifying afternoon that they had been ordered to deliver this message to Count Balsha from one of the flanks of the Albanian army — that was why they hadn't managed to get to him. Everything had collapsed before their eyes, the count's tent kept moving farther and farther away, and the torrent of soldiers had ended up carrying them in the opposite direction. Now, no matter what the cost, they intended to accomplish what they had thus far been prevented from doing: they would find the count, and if they did not find him, then his grave, and there at the grave, even if they were the last men standing, they would deliver their message.

Gjorg followed them with his eyes as they disappeared in a cloud of dust, and an instant later he was convinced that they had been merely an illusion. His spirit was filled with sorrow.

Outside a large village, Gjorg came across a crowd of fugitives moving toward them. He recognized them by their tattered army tunics and the distinctive darkness of their features. They were surprised that in a single day the sun of the Plains of Kosovo had spared their tousled heads but had completely blackened their faces.

Disgraced as they were, they seemed even darker. In three or four languages they hurled curses at the peasants who would not let them into the village, at fate, even at heaven.

"We went to war to save that cross!" they shouted, pointing to the belfry of the village church. "And you won't even give us a crust of bread and shelter for the night! A curse upon you!"

The villagers watched them silently with cold, distrustful eyes. Only the dogs, still tied up, barked and tried to hurl themselves at the strangers.

"May you never live a happy day under your roofs, and may a thornbush blossom by your door!"

Gjorg turned to see who had uttered the curse. He would have recognized Vladan's voice, whether speaking or singing, among dozens of others, but the curse had been uttered somewhere between speech and song.

"Vladan!" he shouted, when he realized it might well have been him.

And it really had been Vladan, his eyes burning with rage, now even gaunter than two days before when they had lost each other during their trek.

Vladan turned around and lifted his hand.

"You see how they treat us!" he said. "These damned spineless, these vile —"

"Hurl curses at them, brother! Hurl curses!" a Hungarian stammered. "Curse them; you know how to curse better than anyone!"

"He knows how to curse because he is a minstrel," said a man in a tattered tunic. "It is his trade both to curse and to exalt."

"Is that so? In this disaster, we Hungarians, more than anyone else, get the short end of the stick! Insults, that's all we get are insults. Yesterday I came across a man, an Albanian I think, who was eating a piece of bread, so I wished him, 'May you get some often!' and do you know what he did? He punched me in the face! As Heaven is my witness, we might have killed each other over these words that offended him. He must have thought they were shameful words and become furious, thinking I was making some improper suggestion!"

Three or four men burst out laughing.

"I think we should head along a different road," the man in the torn tunic said. "You can't expect to see eye to eye with these idiotic peasants."

"They don't want us here," another man said. "But when there is a war to be fought for them, then they want us! When they need to be defended from the Turk or from the devil knows who, then they want us — but ask them for a piece of bread or shelter for the night, and they turn into rabid dogs!"

Vladan continued cursing. He tapped himself, as if fumbling for something.

"You were too quick to throw away your gusla," Gjorg said to himself.

"Let's go," said the man with the torn tunic, not taking his eyes off the dogs.

The fugitives decided to tag along. A little way from the village they sat down to rest beneath some trees.

"You are a minstrel also?" the Hungarian asked Gjorg, eyeing the lahuta slung over his shoulder.

Gjorg nodded.

"Both of us sang in the prince's tent," said Vladan, who lay stretched out next to him. "Yes, on the eve of the battle."

"I have never seen a prince's tent," the Hungarian said. "Tell us what it was like."

Vladan's eyes clouded with pain.

"What can I tell you, Hungarian? They were all there — our Prince Lazar, may he rest in peace, and King Tvrtko, and the lord of the Walachians, and the counts of Albania. They reveled and drank, and sometimes laughed as they listened to our songs."

"But why? Why did they laugh at you?" two or three men asked.

"Not at us," Vladan said sullenly. "No man has ever dared laugh at a minstrel. . . . They were laughing at something else. . . . It is a tangled matter. A Serb or Albanian can understand, but for you it would be too hard. . . . You tell them, Gjorg."

"No, you tell them," Gjorg answered.

Vladan took three or four deep breaths, but then shook his head. It was impossible to explain, he told them, especially now, after the calamity on the Plains of Kosovo. But he continued speaking. "For hundreds of years the evil persisted; what I mean is that Serbian and Albanian songs said exactly the opposite thing . . . particularly when it came to Kosovo, as each side claimed Kosovo as theirs. And each side cursed the other. And this lasted right up to the eve of the battle.

Which was why the princes in the big tent laughed at the songs, for the princes had come together to fight the Turks while the minstrels were still singing songs against one another, the Serbs cursing the Albanians and the Albanians the Serbs. And all the while, across the plain, the Turks were gathering to destroy them both the following day! Lord have mercy upon us!"

Gjorg wanted to tell him that quarrels were always started by those who came last, that when the Serbs had come down from the north, the Albanians had already been there, in Kosovo. But now all of that had become meaningless.

Vladan looked at him as if he had read his mind.

"We ourselves have brought this disaster upon our heads, my brother! We have been fighting and slaughtering each other for so many years over Kosovo, and now Kosovo has fallen to others."

They looked at each other for a few moments

without saying anything, trying to fight back their tears. Now that they were far away from Kosovo, it was as if they had been set free from its shadow. Now their minds could finally shed their fetters, and after their minds, their spirits.

Vladan stared at Gjorg's lahuta.

"Can I try it, brother? My spirit is burning to sing again."

Gjorg stiffened for a moment. He did not know if it was a sin for him to give his lahuta to a Serbian guslar. His memory told him nothing, but the sorrow in the other man's eyes erased his doubts. As if numb, he slipped the strap of his lahuta from his shoulder. Vladan's hand trembled as he took hold of the instrument.

He held it in his hands for a few moments, then his fingers timidly stretched to pluck the single string. Gjorg saw him hold his breath. He was certain that one of two things would happen: either Vladan's hand would not obey the foreign instrument, or the instrument would not obey the foreign hand. The metallic string would snap, or Vladan's fingers would freeze. A split second could bring calamity, and yet, on the other hand, it could also bring harmony.

"This is madness," Gjorg said to himself, as if he were glad. He thought he saw beads of cold sweat on Vladan's brow.

He wanted to tell him not to torture himself this way, or simply to shout, "Don't!" But Vladan had already plucked the string.

For an instant isolated, sorrowful notes rose up. Then came the words. Gjorg saw Vladan's face turn spectral white. And the words, heavy as ancient headstones, were filled with sorrow. "Serbs, to arms! The Albanians are taking Kosovo from us!"

He sang these words, and then dropped his head as if he had been struck. "I cannot! I must not!" he muttered, gasping in despair.

The other fugitives looked at each other, wondering what had happened.

"How wretched we are!" Gjorg said to himself, and yet in his painful words there was a spark of uncertainty. "No, how blessed we are!" And he cried deep inside.

The Serb's eyes were filled with the same tragic lament. Both men were prisoners, tied to each other by ancient chains that they could not and did not want to break.

III

*E*very time they set out to return to the Balkans, they came across people fleeing from there. "Are you out of your minds?" the people said. "We barely got out alive, and you are trying to return? Down there death is everywhere!"

The fleeing people were covered with so much dust that their faces looked more anguished and lifeless than the faces of the saints on the icons they were carrying with them. The news they brought was no less somber: Serbia, it seemed, was in utter disarray. Nobody knew what had become of Walachia or Bosnia. Only half of Albania was still holding out, the western region with its Albano-Venetian castles. And the lands of the Croats and the Slovenes had not yet fallen. But all the Balkan princes, both those in power and those overthrown, had bowed their heads before the Turkish sultan.

"What about Kosovo and its plains?" some of the men asked eagerly.

"Don't ask! Even the grass is gone. Even the blackbirds have fled. Even the name is said to have been changed — it is to be called Muradie from now on, in honor of Sultan Murad, who died there."

"What about the churches?" somebody asked.

"They have been torn down, and temples have been built in their place — they call them mosques, or . . ."

The news about the churches was unclear and contradictory. Some said that only the Serb Orthodox churches had been torn down, while the Catholic churches, those of the Albanians, had been spared. Others insisted that all the churches, Catholic and Orthodox, had been destroyed, and others again claimed the opposite, that not a single church had been touched, and that it was the languages and not the faiths that were under attack.

The people listening clasped their heads in despair. What a calamity! How could people live without their language? How were they to understand each other?

The new arrivals shrugged their shoulders. They had spoken so little during their flight that it seemed they did not see the loss of their language as a big problem. There were even some who felt that it might be better this way. They had said what they had to say in this world, and now that everything had come to an end it was better to be silent.

Others shook their heads doubtfully. The language question was still somehow unsettled, they said. They had heard with their own ears how heralds proclaimed other prohibitions from village to village, prohibitions having to do with chimneys and with women showing their faces.

"No, no!" protested the men, who could not believe what they were hearing. "Prohibiting chimneys and covering women's faces is incredible — it doesn't make sense!"

"Sense or nonsense, call it what you want, but things have changed back there. What's there now is slavery! Do you understand what I am saying? S-l-a-v-e-r-y! I am telling you, there is no more Bosnia, nor Greece, nor Serbia, nor Albania, nor Walachia — only a 'region.' That is what the Turkish officials call the world in their language. For them there are two kinds of regions — good and bad. The good or proper region is the Islamic region. The other is perverse, foreign."

As they spoke they turned to Ibrahim, the Turk they had lost sight of for a few days, who had reappeared the night before.

To their surprise they saw him bowing down,

prostrating himself, as they had heard that Muslims do.

"What are you doing there, Ibrahim?" they called out to him. "You want to become a Christian, and yet you continue to pray like a Muslim?"

The Turk motioned them not to disturb him. He finished his prayers and then got up with a lost look on his face, as if he had returned from another world.

The people stared at him wildly. Whispers were heard: "Accursed Turk!" — "You deceived us all!" — "Right from the start I didn't trust him!"

The Turk looked at them one by one, his eyes surprisingly bright.

"What is wrong?" he asked in a low voice.

"What is wrong?" someone in the crowd shouted. "This morning you made the sign of the cross, and now you pray like a Turk! Are you making fun of us?"

"No, I am not," he answered. "I am not making fun of you. I have an honest heart."

With jumbled words he began telling them his predicament. He wanted to become a Christian from deep within his heart, but at the same time he was unable to expel his other belief. For the time being, both lived within him. Especially at night, he felt them moving, jostling each other, gasping, trying to take over by fair means or foul. So while everyone else was sound asleep, Ibrahim was tortured. He felt that soon enough one of the two faiths would be broken and driven out of him. But he would not pressure or trick either one of them. He was waiting impartially for the result, hoping that in the end the faith of the cross would triumph.

They listened intently, and then a Bosnian man asked him, "In other words, you are waiting for your body to shed one of the faiths like a reptile sheds its skin? Speak frankly, Turk, are you a snake?"

The Turk's eyes filled with deeper sorrow.

"I am not a snake, no! I am an orphan like the stars, a soldier lost like the sands of Yemen, but I am not a snake."

One after the other they turned their backs on him and left. Only a Jew by the name of Heiml stayed back, eyeing him as if he were trying to figure out from which part of the Turk's body one of the two faiths would be expelled.

IV

$\mathcal{N}$ow they were so far away that hardly any news reached them anymore. Even when news did come, it was so altered by the distance that they were not sure what to make of it. It was as if one were to believe a courier who had grown old — even died — traveling down an endless road, had still managed to somehow get through and deliver his message.

This was how the news came to them that their new monarch, who initially had been called "Emir" and then "Sultan," had been given the new title "Yildirim" — "Lightning Bolt."

The fugitives were deeply pained. Under the title of Sultan, he had brought the Balkan and the

Byzantine princes to their knees. With his new title he might well bring all of Europe to its knees. They could get as far away as they wanted; he was bound to follow them. Their souls would be plunged into terror every time the sky darkened and a lightning bolt came tearing through driving rain.

A second message specified that Lightning Bolt was only the nickname of Bayezid, the new monarch who had mounted the throne after his father's death on the Plains of Kosovo. But this new message, instead of erasing the first one, gave it even more weight.

The Turks, before they ground the world under their heel, would conquer the skies. They had put the crescent moon on their banners and then made thunder and lightning their own — and tomorrow God knows what they would attack: the stars, the winter clouds, perhaps time itself.

For a few days the fugitives stayed in a friendly region. The villagers gave them bread to eat and listened to their tales with compassion even though they did not understand their language, and at night they let them sleep in the porches of their churches. The villagers feared only one thing: that the refugees might have brought the plague with them. The rest did not matter.

They had heard talk about the Turkish peril, but only vaguely. And for some time now there had been talk of a new crusade being summoned against the Turk. All the Christian states were to rally together. The pope of Rome himself was to head the crusade.

The fugitives rejoiced at these words. The farther north they went, the higher the cathedrals and the towers of the castles became. Black iron crosses dominated the skies. One stifling night, two solitary lightning bolts, instead of sending shivers through the crosses as one would expect, seemed to turn in terror and dash away.

God be praised — Christianity was still mighty in all its lands. The Balkans had been defeated on the continent's borders, but here, in its heart, things were quite different. The fugitives were soothed by the city gates and walled towers, the princely titles and emblems and coats of arms, and the Latin inscriptions in the bronze and marble of the churches.

While the fugitives were awaiting permission to enter one of the somber little cities (at times their very lack of size seemed to make them all the more dismal), guards came and dragged Ibrahim the Turk away and clapped him in irons.

At first they were not particularly worried. They had often run into trouble on account of the Turk. But this time things looked bad. All the explanations about how he had deserted his own army and how he had two faiths were of no avail. Quite the opposite. Every time his two faiths were mentioned, the guards' eyes flashed with scorn. In the end, the Balkan fugitives were told that they were wasting their time: the Turk would be submitted to a secret investigation by the Holy Inquisition.

"If he is innocent," they told each other, "then

he will be set free like all the other innocents, but he might well be a spy, and we in our foolishness may have been gullible." Others recalled that it was not the Holy Inquisition that dealt with spies but the town court. "If you ask me, I never really liked this business of his two faiths," one of the Walachians said. "A man cannot have two faiths, just as no creature of God can have two heads. There might be two-headed vipers, but no two-headed men."

The trial that began two weeks later confirmed what the Walachian had said. It was his double faith, even his triple faith — brought to light under torture — that cost the Turk his neck. During the trial, he asserted that he had wanted to become a Christian upon seeing the cross above the Plains of Kosovo. But the Islamic faith was not prepared to leave his body without a struggle, which was why he continued praying to his prophet. "And why are you drawn to the Jewish faith? Are not the other two enough for you, eh?" the judge yelled.

A faint murmur rose from the crowd.

The Turk tried to explain that he had only listened to Heiml the Jew out of curiosity, but the crowd was already growing wild.

He was to be burned at the stake, for it was certain that he had entered into a pact with the devil. "Had he kept to his Muslim belief, he would have remained unscathed," the judge pronounced. "And had he converted to our faith, we would have welcomed him with open arms, like a brother. But he did neither the one nor the other," the judge continued. "He has attempted to do the impossible, to waver between two faiths, doubtless following the devil's counsel."

The judge spoke at length of the holy and immutable principles of the church. The antichrist was attacking from all sides, but the church was unshakable. The creation of men of two faiths was only the most recent of Satan's inventions.

The judge glared menacingly at the small group of Balkan men who were huddling together like sheep, and spoke harsh words of warning to those who undertook to turn Europe's Christian traditions into pagan infamy.

The Turk was burned in front of the cathedral the following day at noon. As the smoke began to envelope the convicted man, the others remembered the day before the battle, back on the Plains of Kosovo, when both sides had unleashed curtains of smoke so that they would not have to look at each other.

The Turk's first cries came from within the smoke. Incomprehensible words, it seemed, in his language. The crowd tried to detect the word "Allah," the only word they knew, but the convicted man did not pronounce it.

The inquisitor who had prosecuted the burning man craned his neck so he could hear better. "I think he said 'Abracadabra,' " he whispered to his deputy.

The other man nodded, "I believe he did." And he raised his iron cross like a shield.

"The poor Turk!" one of the Bosnians said to

his friends. "He is crying for his mother. Remember when he told us that *mama* in his language is *abllà?*"

"No, I don't remember a thing!" The other man cut him short.

The Turk's shouts turned into stifled moans; then he emitted a sudden and terrible "*NON!*" It was an isolated shout, completely different from his previous cries, although that might only have been because it was the only Latin word he said. It was probably the first word he had learned in the Christian world, and in leaving that world, which had not accepted him, he expressed his regret in that final shout.

V

*A*fter the Turk was burned, the Balkan fugitives left immediately and headed north, out of fear that the Inquisition would pursue everyone in any way connected with him. The principalities they crossed became increasingly small and austere. It was as if an ancient fury had shriveled their lands and towers, while the swords of the guardsmen seemed increasingly sharp.

There were more and more searches. The fugitives were searched for hidden icons, for symptoms of the plague, for counterfeit currency. Most of the people had never heard of the Battle of Kosovo, so when the fugitives spoke of it, they aroused suspicion instead of compassion. Quite often they were told that if they were really soldiers, they should enlist as mercenaries in one of the many local regiments. There was no lack of wrangling princes and counts. The counts in particular were, more often than not, extremely belligerent and ever ready to hire ruthless warriors.

The fugitives listened in bewilderment. After the calamity of Kosovo, they could not face another war of any kind. They would rather work for blacksmiths or cheese makers. They knew how to make a type of cheese that, from what they could tell, was unknown in these parts. They also knew how to turn milk into yogurt, which was tangy, fresh, and did not spoil for days.

In the beginning, the villagers were amazed at this yogurt but then suddenly became terrified that they might find themselves burned at the stake. They quickly poured the "diseased" milk out of their jugs, and with tears in their eyes begged the Balkans not to breathe a word of this to anyone, as it would mean certain death for all concerned.

They passed through villages where different languages were spoken. One day Hans, a simpleton who tagged along part of the way, eyeing Gjorg's lahuta, asked him, full of curiosity, what that "thingamajig" slung over his shoulder was. Gjorg was about to explain, but Hans shook his head slyly — "I know what it is! It is the instrument with which you turn milk into yogurt, ha, ha, ha!"

Gjorg laughed too, but Vladan, who had heard Hans, looked at them sullenly.

"You must throw that lahuta away, or you might well end up burned at the stake."

"I will throw it away," Gjorg said. "I will find a faraway, secluded spot, I shall play it one last time, and then I will throw it away."

And he would surely have thrown it away, had not something extraordinary happened at the end of that week. Gjorg, Vladan, and Manolo, a Walachian storyteller, were summoned to a castle. The messengers who brought them the invitation told them that their lord always invited

French and German minstrels to his banquets, and that he had heard about them and was interested in listening to their songs.

Gjorg was deep in thought; Vladan was on the verge of tears because he no longer had his gusla. As for Manolo — his face turned yellow and he wanted to run away, but the others managed with great difficulty to persuade him not to disgrace them.

Somehow Vladan succeeded in making a gusla by the day of the banquet. "Don't worry!" the others said to him. "If worse comes to worst, you can use Gjorg's lahuta."

They placed all their hopes on this banquet. Now respect for them was bound to grow. People would see that they were good for more than just making war and cheese and "diseased" milk, that they could also sing of great deeds, just as their ancient clansmen had. Their situation would perhaps improve, suspicions would be dispelled, and perhaps they would even be granted permission to settle down in this place.

The Balkan fugitives escorted the minstrels part of the way and bade them good luck. Bathed and combed, their faces tense with agitation, the three of them, together with a Croat who could mimic the calls of birds and wolves, disappeared through the castle's heavy portal.

The Balkan fugitives crossed themselves three times; some of them fell to their knees; others prayed with burning fervor: "Do not abandon us, Holy Mary, Mother of God!"

VI

A dozen minstrels waited in a row for their turn. The French sang of Roland, their hero who had blown his horn before dying, and the Germans sang of the ring of their lord whose name was Siegfried. Another minstrel, who seemed to be neither German nor French, sang of a Vilhelm who had shot an arrow at an apple he had placed on his son's head.

When their turn came, the lord of the castle announced to his company that they were going to hear the Balkan minstrels who had come straight from the Battle of Kosovo, where the Turks had dealt Christendom a bitter blow. "Let us all hope and pray that this blow will be the last!"

One after the other, in the heavy silence, they sang their songs, ancient and cold as stone, each in his own language: "A great fog is covering the Field of the Blackbirds! Rise, O Serbs, the Albanians are taking Kosovo." "A black fog has descended —Albanians, to arms, Kosovo is falling to the damned Serb."

The guests, who had been listening with sorrowful faces, asked the Balkan minstrels to explain what their songs were about. At first the nobles sat speechless, not believing what they were told. Then they became angry — the Balkan lands have fallen, and these minstrels continue singing songs that keep the old enmities alive?

"It is true that there is dissension everywhere, but dissension like yours is really unique in the world!" one of the guests said contemptuously.

"What wretches you are!" the lord of the castle shouted.

They stood with bowed heads as the guests

denounced them. They would have tried to explain, as they had that evening long ago, but they realized that their words would fall on deaf ears. "It would have been better for us to have died on the battlefield than end up at this cursed banquet," Gjorg thought.

Among the hosts sat an old woman, who peered at them intently. From her attire and her position at the table, it was obvious that she was a great lady. Her eyes were fiery, but her face was white and cold, as if it were from another world.

"You must sing of other things," she said in a kindly voice.

The minstrels held their peace.

"What songs do you expect from them?" one of the guests at the end of the table asked. "Hate is all they know!"

"They corrupt everything, the way they corrupt the milk," a guest shouted through the mocking laughter.

"Do not insult them," the old woman said, her eyes fixed on Gjorg's hand, which was clenching the hilt of his dagger. "In their land," she continued, "insulting a guest is a black calamity, blacker than a lost war."

Silence descended on the banquet.

"Take your hand off your dagger," Vladan whispered. "This can cost us our necks." Entreaties and pleas rained down on Gjorg's head like an avalanche of rocks: "Don't do anything foolish that will cost us all our necks!" On the verge of tears, he pulled his numb fingers from the hilt of his dagger.

"At our table no man shall offend another!" the lord of the castle said.

The old woman's eyes became even kindlier.

"If you cannot sing or do not want to, then why do you not tell us a tale?" she asked. "I have heard that there is much of interest in the lands from which you come. Tell us of the living, of the dead, of those hovering in between."

Vladan looked at Manolo and then at the Croat, as if he were seeking help, but both men shrugged their shoulders. It was not surprising that they wavered — the one could only tell folk-tales, the other only mimic the calls of birds and wolves. To ask these minstrels to talk of their lands was like asking a cavalryman to take a broom and sweep the road. And yet, a large crowd of Balkan fugitives outside the castle gates had placed all their hope in them.

Vladan began speaking spontaneously. He himself was amazed that he could. It was the first time that he did not sing before listeners, but speak. It seemed ridiculous, shameful, and sinful, all together. Two or three times he felt that his mouth was about to dry up. "Do not stop, brother!" the others urged him with their eyes, but he signaled to them that he was at the end of his tether. The others came to his rescue. The first to speak was Manolo the Walachian, then the Croat, and finally Gjorg, who, after the insult he had suffered, had seemed determined not to open his mouth, even on pain of death.

Their tales were wondrous, at times cruel and chilling and at times filled with sorrow. Everyone listened, but the great lady most intently. Her face was still a mask, but her eyes were on fire. "These tales bring to mind the Greek tragedies," she said in a low voice. "They are of the same diamond dust, the same seed."

"What are these Greek tragedies?" the lord of the castle asked.

She sighed deeply and said that they were perhaps the greatest wealth of mankind. A simple treasure chest, like the one in which any feudal lord hides his gold coins, was big enough to hold all these tragedies. And yet, not only had they not been preserved, but over the centuries they had been scattered, these tragedies that would have made the world — in other words, its spirit — twice as beautiful.

The lord of the castle shook his head, dumbfounded at the thought of such negligence. The old lady smiled sadly. How could she explain to him that she, too, had always felt the same way about the negligence of the erudite men, the monastic librarians, the scribes and abbots? She had written countless letters to princes, cardinals, even to the pope. The responses she received had been increasingly cool, until finally she was openly reproached: instead of devoting herself to Jesus Christ, she, an erudite lady, possibly the most erudite lady of all the French and German lands, was obsessed with pagan gods.

For days in a row she had swept through her vast library like a shadow. But it became rapidly clear that there was no place in heaven for ancient deities.

Now, after so many years, she had heard as if in a trance these thunderclaps from that distant world, brought by these destitute fugitives with faces wild from war. Thunderclaps like fragments of the crown fallen from the ancient sky. Rites of death, changes of season, sacrificial customs, tales of blood feuds — all carrying the malediction for a thousand years, more immaculately than any chronicle.

Now, in those lands from which these poor destitute men had come, there were no ancient theaters left, no tragedies. There were only scattered fragments. Now that night had descended on all those lands, perhaps the time had come for her to resume her letters. That region, which seemed to be but a distant forecourt of Europe, was in fact its bridal chamber. The roots that had given birth to everything were there. And therefore it should under no circumstances be abandoned.

The Balkan minstrels continued to tell their tales, now interrupting each other. In their desire to be accepted they had forgotten the insults, and humbly, almost awkwardly, begged: *We want to be like you. We think like you. Don't drive us away.*

The old lady sensed that there was something missing from their tales.

"Could you sing the things you have been telling us?" she asked.

They were shaken as if they had been dealt a blow. Then, tearing themselves out of their stupor, one after the other, each in his own language, and finally in Latin, said "No." *Non*.

"Why not?" she asked kindly. "Why do you not try?"

"*Non, domina magna,* we cannot under any circumstances. We are minstrels of war."

She shook her head and then insistently, almost beseeching them, repeated her request.

The Balkan minstrels' faces grew dark. They broke out in cold sweats, as if they were being tortured. Even the words they uttered were uttered as if in a nightmare. They were martial minstrels. They were filled with fervor and hatred, but there was something vital missing. They could not break out of the mold. Besides which, they would first have to consult their elders. Consult the dead. They would have to wait for them to appear in their dreams so that they could consult them. No, they could not, under any circumstances. *Non*.

VII

The last sounds dissolved into the night, the barking of the dogs thinned out, but the great lady could not fall asleep. After a banquet, sleep always came either far too easily or with too much difficulty. And yet, her insomnia that night was of a different kind. Among the thoughts that always came to plague her, a new one appeared — solitary, foreign, and dangerous as a winter wolf. This thought, alien to her mind, to the whole world perhaps, tried to take shape but immediately disintegrated, thrashing around as if in a trap, tearing out of its confines, but then, on gaining its freedom the thought fled, rushing back into its snare, the skull from which it had escaped.

A courtyard with an unhinged door, a Mongol spear, and a map of the continent sent recently from Amsterdam struggled to connect with each other.

The old lady finally got out of bed, threw something over her shoulders, and walked over to the window. The thought that had repelled her sleep was still sparkling in her mind, formless and without a protective crust, free and lethal.

Standing by the big window, she finally managed to calm somewhat the foaming fury. She coaxed it tenderly, in the hope that it would rise from the fog.

And that is exactly what happened. The map and the barbarian spear with its tufts of fur and the mysterious inscriptions on its shaft connected with each other. The whole European continent was there: the lands of the Gauls, the German regions, and, farther up, the Baltic territories and the rugged Scandinavian lands sprawled out like a sleeping lion. Then, below the central flatlands, the peninsulas of the Pyrenees, the Apennines, and the third peninsula, which had initially been named Illyricum and Byzantium and now was being called "Balkan." She saw clearly the regions from which the poor wandering fugitives had come: Croatia, Albania, Serbia, Greece, Bosnia, Walachia, Macedonia. From now on they would have to carry this new name, fossilized and ponderous, on their backs like a curse as they stumbled along like a tortoise in its shell.

The barbarian spear had always been like a sign at the borders of the continent, but they had been quick to forget, like a nightmare that scatters with the approach of dawn. This is how they had all forgotten Attila and Genghis Khan, and this was perhaps how they were going to forget the Ottomans.

"Your apprehension is a great surprise to me," Baron Melanchthon had said to her a few months earlier. "You are worried about something that does not exist, and therefore cannot be threatened. Europe — Asia — are but entities in the barbarians' minds, or on their parchments. They are figures of legend, half woman, half God knows what."

She had taken offense and made no reply.

"How dreadful," she said to herself, her eyes fixed on the darkness as if she were speaking to the night. "The Ottomans have burst into the outer court of their mansion and they look the other way. They are reinforcing the gates of their castles, posting more guards on their towers, but when it comes to looking farther, their eyes are blind."

"Europe," she said to herself, as if she were trying to seize this word transformed by ridicule and neglect. She had watched words wilt away and die when they were neglected by the minds of men. "Europe," she repeated, almost with dread. Twenty-odd empires, a hundred different peoples. Some jammed against each other, others far apart. Which was Europe's true mass — constricted or distended? As learned friends of hers had explained, Europe had started out as a dense galaxy in the middle of a void, but in recent years, particularly with the great plague, it had turned into a void itself, besieged by great hordes.

The barbarians had again burst through the defending barriers. They brandished their spears right under Europe's nose without clarifying the meaning of their sign: death or goodwill.

One by one she brought to mind her powerful connections: princes, cardinals, philosophers, even the pope of Rome. She tried to recollect their faces, their eyes, particularly the lines on their foreheads, where the worries of a man are drawn more clearly than anywhere else. Were they racking their brains how to rally together to defend themselves, particularly now that their southern barrier had been breached, or were they thinking no further than their next banquet?

Her weary mind found calm. Then, in her thoughts, she saw a long rope, an exceedingly long rope, uncoil as if it had been randomly thrown. "Greece!" she exclaimed, as if she had had a revelation. Her friend Wyclif had told her that this had been how the ancient Greek world had measured itself: an endless strip of land, a thousand five hundred miles long, stretching from the coasts of Asia Minor to the Greek peninsula and the shores of Illyria, and from the southern beaches of Gaul down to Calabria and Sicily. This rope was delicate, brittle, cut in places by waves of fate, and yet it had managed to hold out and penetrate the depths of the continent.

Now the Greeks, like the other peoples of the region, had been toppled. The eleven peoples of the peninsula had to stumble along within a communal shell named *Balkan,* and it seemed that nobody gave them a second thought, unless to anathematize them: "You cursed wretches!"

She could not blot out the eyes of the poor destitute fugitives who had sung and spoken at the banquet. In their black sockets she saw a Europe that had died, transformed into a doleful memory. "Great Lord in Heaven! Why have you wrought these things in those lands?" she thought. "One has to lose a thing in order to cherish it!"

Everything they had narrated unraveled

slowly in her mind: the sacrifices at the foot of bridges, the Furies in the guise of washerwomen on the banks of a river, the idlers in the village coffeehouses, the killer forced to attend the funeral feast of his victim. "It is all there, O Lord!" she gasped. "Fragments of the great ruins that gave birth to everything!"

"We must not abandon our outer court!" she almost said aloud. "If it falls, we shall all fall!"

Her mind tumbled once more into an unbearable whirl. Her head and temples ached viciously. She tried to rise; she even thought she *had* risen, found paper and pen to write to princes, to her friend Wyclif, even the pope of Rome. And she felt much lighter, not only able to write but ready to deliver her message with her own hands across the sky.

In the morning she was found dead and cold. A whiteness, which one only finds in the darkness of nonexistence, had settled on her face like a mask.

All the banquet guests of the previous night attended her majestic funeral, which took place in the neighboring principality from which she had come. After the mass and the ringing of the bells, someone remembered to summon the foreign minstrels. It seems that during the banquet she had said that she would like them to sing something at her grave.

They numbly took out their musical instruments and, with the same numbness, sang a song for her. "A black fog has descended, the great lady has died. Rise, O Serbs, the Albanians are seizing Kosovo!" — "A black fog has descended upon us, the great lady has died. Rise, O Albanians! Kosovo is falling to the pernicious Serb!"

They sang, and even though the mourners at the funeral did not understand the words, they listened with full attention, their eyes blank, sorrowful, and filled with incomprehension.

The Royal Prayer

As the army prepared to set out on its homeward march with my body, leaving behind only my blood gathered in a leaden vessel, I felt for a while that the world had fallen silent forever. But then I heard the rumbling of the iron chariots and the trampling of hooves growing fainter in the distance, and I realized that I had been left here on my own.

I had heard my father say, as he had heard his father say, that all aberration, memory, fury, and vengeance are imprinted in a man's blood. And yet it seems that I was the first monarch whose blood was so violently pressed out of his body on these cursed plains.

My corpse — limbs, crowned head, hair, my gray chest with the wound in its center — was carried to Anatolia, taking nothing with it. Everything remained here, and I have come to believe that my viziers did this to elude the shadow of my blood.

Thus they left, abandoning me here in this tomb, with an oil lamp above me burning day and night. I thought they would be quick to return, to attack Europe, now that the road lay open, or at least to pay homage to me, to show that they had not forgotten me. But spring came and went, as did summer, and then another spring, but no one came.

Where were they; what were they doing? Three years passed, seven, thirteen. Here and there a lone traveler stopping at my tomb brought me smatterings of news from the world. I wanted to shout, "Serves you right, Bayezid my son!" when I heard that Tamerlane had battled his way into Ankara and locked him in an iron cage like a savage beast.

So this was the reason why they had stayed away so long. My curse had struck my son who had killed his brother, Yakub, and perhaps even me, to seize my throne.

When there is no hope, time passes so much more slowly than when hope exists. Blood does not lose its power as it congeals. Even dry, powdered over the sides of the leaden vessel, it grows only wilder.

A curse upon you, people of the Balkans, who charged me to set out in my old age and lay down my life on these plains! Above all, a curse upon you for my solitude!

The twentieth year passed, and still there was no news. The twenty-fifth year. The fortieth. I had begun to believe that all had been lost forever, when I heard a familiar rumbling clatter. When peoples are preparing for battle against one another there is no mistaking the signs. "Here they come!" I said. "Here come my Turks!" New commanders will have arisen, new viziers, and, needless to say, a new generation of men. I was ready to offer my death to my people, to give them my blessing, when I realized that these were not Turks approaching.

The Balkan peoples were out to slaughter each other on the Plains of Kosovo. This time Serbs and Albanians had hoisted their emblems: the Albanians the Catholic cross, the Serbs the Orthodox.

"Butcher each other, you Balkan savages!" I muttered, renewing my curse on them.

But even without my curse they were determined to trample one another into the ground. They had set out on this course of destruction six hundred, seven hundred years before my campaign. They had reached a temporary truce in these flatlands only to resume their terrible slaughter even more viciously than before.

I must say I felt great joy at hearing them taunt each other. But soon enough my joy began to fade. Their fury was so protracted that even I, an outsider, grew weary.

Many years passed this way. Seventy, then a

hundred and seventy. The oil lamp with its dim flame burned and burned in my tomb. New sultans with ancient, ever-recurring names appeared — Mehmet, Murad, Sulejman, Ahmet, Murad, Mehmet — only to fall, one after the other, into oblivion. They had managed to bring half of Europe to its knees, but now, weary, they began to fall back. The Christian cross turned out to be more powerful than it had seemed. Our crescent withdrew from Vienna, the Hungarian flatlands, somber Poland, Ukraine, Crimea, and finally the Balkan lands, which I believe we had loved the most. Perhaps we picked up the Balkan people's madness and they picked up our sluggishness. In the end we parted forever, each to our own destiny.

I remained more solitary than ever, with the pale flame of the oil lamp above me, a sorrowful crown.

And the Balkans, instead of trying to build something together, attacked each other again like beasts freed from their iron chains. Their songs were as wild as their weapons. And the prophecies and proclamations were terrible. "For seven hundred years I shall burn your towers! You dogs! For seven hundred years I shall cut you down!" the minstrels sang. And what they declared in their songs was inevitably done, and what was done was then added to their songs, as poison is added to poison.

Time has flown. Five hundred years passed since the day I fell. Then five hundred seventy. Then six hundred. I am still here, alone in my tomb with the flame of the charred oil lamp, while their din, like the roar of the sea, never ends.

From time to time the wind brings shreds of tattered newspaper thrown away by travelers. From these I learn what is going on all around. The surprising names of viziers and countries: NATO. R. Cook. Madeleine Albright. The slaughter of children in Drenicë. Milosevic. *Mein Kampf*. Again the name of the woman vizier. At times, my name, too, appears amongst theirs: Murad I.

Allah, I have been so tired for over six hundred years now, a Muslim monarch all alone in the middle of the vast Christian expanses. During my worst hours I am seized by the suspicion that maybe my blood is the origin of all this horror. I know this is a crazed suspicion, and yet, in this nonexistence in which I am, I beg you: Finally grant me oblivion, my Lord! Make them remove my blood from these cold plains. And not just the leaden vessel, but make them dig up the earth around where my tent stood, where drops of my blood spattered the ground. O Lord, hear my prayer! Take away all the mud around here, for even a few drops of blood are enough to hold all the memory of the world.